Field-Trip Fiasco

Julie Danneberg

Illustrated by Judy Love

Charlesbridge

*Many thanks to all the teachers and students
at Falcon Creek Middle School. You are the best!*
—J. D.

*In memory of my mother, Dorothy Love,
master of the Family Field Trip.*
—J. L.

Text copyright © 2015 by Julie Danneberg
Illustrations copyright © 2015 by Judy Love

Published by Charlesbridge
85 Main Street
Watertown, MA 02472
(617) 926-0329
www.charlesbridge.com

Library of Congress Cataloging-in-Publication Data
Danneberg, Julie, 1958–author.
 Field-trip fiasco/Julie Danneberg; illustrated by Judy Love.
  pages cm
 Summary: Mrs. Hartwell is taking her class on a field trip to
the zoo, and because of the fiasco last time she has prepared a list
of tips to deal with anticipated disasters—but will they work?
 ISBN 978-1-58089-671-9 (reinforced for library use)
 ISBN 978-1-58089-672-6 (softcover)
 ISBN 978-1-60734-760-6 (ebook)
 ISBN 978-1-60734-717-0 (ebook pdf)
1. School field trips—Juvenile fiction. 2. Zoos—Juvenile fiction.
3. Elementary school teachers—Juvenile fiction. 4. Elementary
schools—Juvenile fiction. [1. School field trips—Fiction.
2. Zoos—Fiction. 3. Teachers—Fiction. 4. Schools—Fiction.]
I. Love, Judith DuFour, illustrator. II. Title.

PZ7.D2327Fh 2015
813.6—dc23   2013049023

Printed in China
(hc) 10 9 8 7 6 5 4 3 2 1
(sc) 10 9 8 7 6 5 4 3 2 1

Illustrations done on Strathmore Series 500 Bristol with black ink and transparent dyes
Display type hand-lettered by Judy Love
Text type set in Electra LH by Linotype-Hell AG
Color separations by KHL Chroma Graphics, Singapore
Manufactured by C & C Offset Printing Co. Ltd. in Shenzhen, Guangdong, China
Production supervision by Brian G. Walker
Designed by Diane M. Earley

It was the morning of the field trip to the zoo. Mrs. Hartwell's students tumbled into the classroom. They were very, very, very excited.

Mrs. Hartwell, however, shuffled in slowly. She remembered the last field trip.

It took a little bit of rest, and a little bit of time, and a lot of research, but eventually Mrs. Hartwell was ready to try again.

The morning of the field trip she wrote out her very own list of field-trip tips and put together her handy-dandy, just-in-case-something-unexpected-happens bag. Mrs. Hartwell felt ready for anything.

During circle time Mrs. Hartwell helped her students get ready. "When does the fun start?" Andy asked.

"Getting organized is fun," Mrs. Hartwell said, smiling. "Speaking of fun, let's review your learning task for the zoo. Who can tell me what it is?"

"We're supposed to be animal observers," Madison called out.

"And write down what we see animals doing," Alexandra added.

"That doesn't sound like fun," Andy complained.

"It'll be great! We'll all be focused and learn lots," Mrs. Hartwell said as she passed out the animal-observation sheets.

Foolproof Field-Trip Tip #1: Give students a job to keep them focused and learning... and out of trouble!

"Can I go to the bathroom?" Eddie asked just as he got to the bus.

"Hurry back," Mrs. Hartwell said distractedly as she assigned everyone their seats.

"Darn!" Andy said, when he saw where he was seated.

Mrs. Hartwell felt good. She felt prepared. She felt relieved that they'd gotten this far without any problems. As the bus began to pull away from the curb, Mrs. Hartwell looked over her list again.

"STOP!" she yelled, running down the aisle.

Mrs. Hartwell hurried off the bus, into the school, and almost into the boys' bathroom.

The bus bounced along the highway. Mrs. Hartwell was happy. Her students were happy, too.

All of a sudden, instead of bouncing, the bus chugged. And then instead of chugging, it stopped.

"No problem," Mrs. Hartwell thought. She pulled out a huge bag of animal crackers from her just-in-case bag. Everyone agreed that being stuck on the bus was the absolutely perfect way to start a field trip.

Soon enough the bus was fixed, and they arrived at the zoo. Mrs. Hartwell lined up everyone by partner and asked them to count off by twos. The class counted all the way to twenty-six.

"Twenty-six?!" Mrs. Hartwell exclaimed when they stopped. "But we only have twenty-four students in our class! Who's in our class who's *not* in our class?"

Jack and Alexandra brought two little boys up to the front of the line.

After a quick look around, Mrs. Hartwell returned the boys to their teacher.

Foolproof Field-Trip Tip #4:
Partnering up prevents problems.

Mrs. Hartwell's class started at the petting zoo.

"Don't forget to fill in your observation sheet," she reminded everyone.

"The goat has a beard and looks like an old man," Alexandra wrote as she walked. She didn't see the hay bale until she somersaulted over it. OUCH!

Madison didn't see Alexandra until she somersaulted over her. OUCH!

Mrs. Hartwell gave a few hugs as she hustled her students away from the petting zoo. "Just because you're observing the animals doesn't mean you can stop observing where you're going," she reminded everyone.

Foolproof Field-Trip Tip #5:
Bring a first-aid kit with lots of bandages.

"Don't forget your observation sheets," Mrs. Hartwell called out when they got to the elephant compound.

"The mama elephant is standing quietly with her baby," Alexandra wrote.

"The baby elephant has his eyes closed. I bet he's sleeping," Madison wrote.

"This is boring. They aren't doing anything. There is nothing to write," Eddie wrote.

Everyone was so busy writing that no one noticed
the daddy elephant take a big, long, thirsty drink.

SPRAY. SPLASH. SPLATTER.

All the students screamed.

Eddie screamed the loudest. "I didn't see him coming," he moaned.

"Hmmmm," thought Mrs. Hartwell as she dried Eddie off and helped him put on some new clothes.

Foolproof Field-Trip Tip #6:
Bring lots of paper towels and an extra tee shirt.

The aviary was the next stop.

"This is like walking into a giant bird cage!" Jack yelled.

"Write it on your observation sheet," Mrs. Hartwell reminded him.

Everyone looked around quickly and then got busy writing.

They were so busy writing that they didn't see the
baby birds peeking out of the nest above the door.
And they didn't notice the sparrows taking a bath.
    But they did hear the parrot squawk as it flew
over Eddie . . .

. . . and they observed something wet and white drop onto his head.

And they watched Eddie jumping up and down, yelling, "Gross! Yuck! Get it off me!"

But even after Mrs. Hartwell wet-wiped and paper-toweled him off, Eddie was still howling.

That's when the zookeeper appeared and said with a
smile, "Did you know that many people consider an
accident like this a sign of good luck? Congratulations!"
He handed Eddie a special badge and a free pass
to the zoo.

Eddie stopped screaming. He smiled.

"Why does all of the good stuff always
happen to Eddie?" Andy asked loudly.

And that gave Mrs. Hartwell an idea.

"Class, Eddie's good luck is going to rub off on all of us. Put away your observation sheets. For the rest of the day, we'll continue to be animal observers, but we'll be animal-observation *writers* later!"

"Yeah!" everyone cheered as they put away their observation sheets and headed out to see the rest of the zoo.

The monkeys chattered. And so did the students.

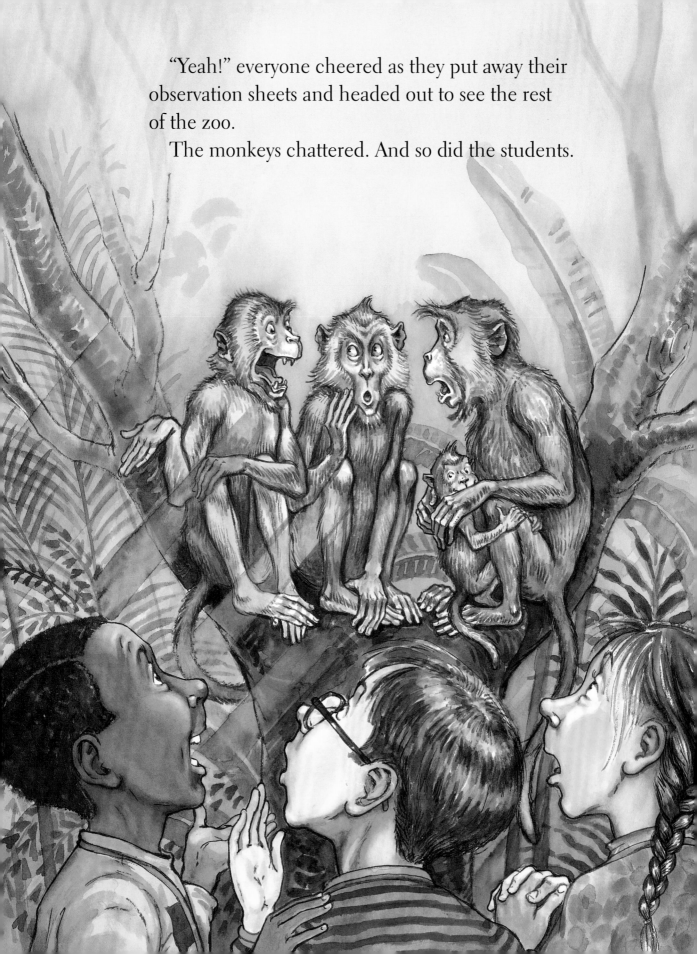

The lions roared. And so did the students.

The hyenas laughed. And so did the students.
Throughout the rest of the day, the students
noticed everything.

When they got back to school, Mrs. Hartwell's class filled out the rest of their animal-observation sheets. They had so much to write and talk about. They had learned a lot on their field trip to the zoo.

And so had Mrs. Hartwell.